For information address Disney • Lucasfilm Press,
1101 Flower Street, Glendale, California 91201.

Printed in China
First Hardcover Edition, July 2016   10 9 8 7 6 5 4 3 2

ISBN 978-1-4847-8667-3
FAC-023680-17198

Visit the official *Star Wars* website at: www.starwars.com

Escape from the Death Star

Disney · LUCASFILM PRESS

Los Angeles • New York

Book Three

L uke Skywalker, Han Solo, and Chewbacca had done what seemed impossible: they had rescued the rebel leader Princess Leia from her prison on board the Empire's space station—the Death Star. But now they faced what might be an even bigger challenge: getting past the stormtroopers who stood between them and their ship, the *Millennium Falcon*.

While his young friends were rescuing Leia, Obi-Wan Kenobi's mission was to turn off the tractor beam that kept the *Millennium Falcon* trapped on the Death Star.

Using his mastery of the Force, Obi-Wan made the stormtroopers guarding the tractor beam think they had heard a noise. When they looked away to see what was going on, Obi-Wan turned it off!

Now Obi-Wan just had to get back to the ship and he and his friends could get away from the Death Star!

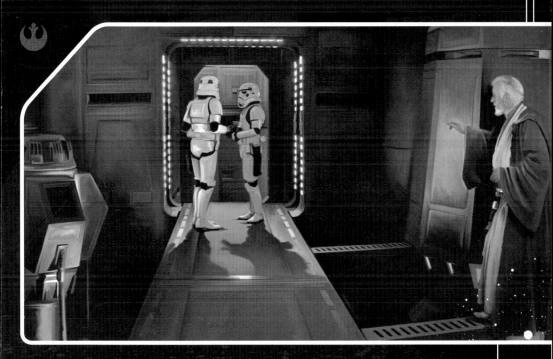

Meanwhile, Luke and the others crept up to a window overlooking the captive *Millennium Falcon*. Han hated to see his ship grounded and surrounded by stormtroopers.

"You came in that thing?" asked Leia, surprised at the *Millennium Falcon*'s beat-up condition. "You're braver than I thought."

Using his com-link, Luke called the droids C-3PO and R2-D2 and told them to meet the others by the ship. But before his group could take more than a few steps, a patrol of stormtroopers spotted them. Raising their blasters, the stormtroopers attacked!

"Get back to the ship!" Han yelled as he and Chewbacca ran toward the stormtroopers, firing their weapons.

Luke and Leia ran toward the *Falcon*'s docking bay. But when they turned the corner, another platoon of stormtroopers was waiting for them!

The pair tried to escape through a door, but instead they found a gap that was too big to jump across.

"I think we took a wrong turn!" Luke shouted.

With the stormtroopers approaching, Luke blasted the door's controls, sealing it shut behind him and Leia.

Leia knew the door wouldn't hold off the troopers for long. She and Luke needed to get to the other side of the gap. "Quick!" she yelled. "Find the controls that extend the bridge."

Luke looked at the smoking switch panel beside the door. "I think I just blasted it."

With time running out, Luke looked through his belt and found a grappling hook. He quickly looped it around a pipe overhead.

Luke lifted Leia in his arms. She kissed him on the cheek for luck before they swung across to the other side.

Luke and Leia were safe, but the stormtroopers were still chasing Han and Chewie! As the pair ran down a long hallway, the stormtroopers tried to cut off their escape route by closing a set of thick blast doors.

With a burst of speed, Chewbacca and Han raced through the closing doors with only seconds to spare. Now it was the stormtroopers who were caught on the wrong side of the sealed doors!

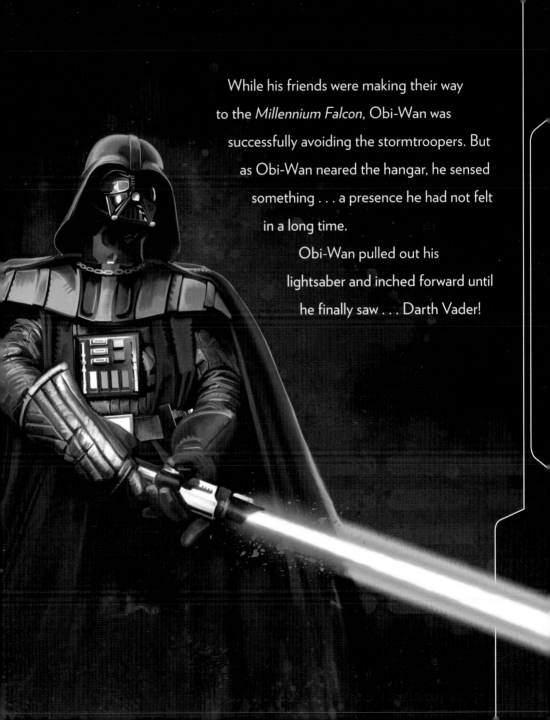

While his friends were making their way to the *Millennium Falcon*, Obi-Wan was successfully avoiding the stormtroopers. But as Obi-Wan neared the hangar, he sensed something . . . a presence he had not felt in a long time.

Obi-Wan pulled out his lightsaber and inched forward until he finally saw . . . Darth Vader!

The Dark Lord of the Sith stood with his red lightsaber drawn. "I've been waiting for you, Obi-Wan," he said. "When I left you, I was but the learner. Now I am the master."

"Only a master of evil," Obi-Wan replied.

As Vader attacked, Obi-Wan wielded his own lightsaber, moving with the ease and speed of a Jedi Knight.

But Vader was more physically powerful than the Jedi Master, and he soon gained the advantage over Obi-Wan.

"Your powers are weak, old man," Vader taunted.

The Jedi Knight was unafraid. "You can't win, Darth."

"You should not have come back," Vader replied in a deep, threatening voice.

In the hangar, Luke and Leia caught up with Chewbacca and Han. R2-D2 and C-3PO arrived moments later.

Just steps away, Obi-Wan was still fighting Darth Vader, their lightsabers crackling as they connected.

Out of the corner of his eye, Obi-Wan saw that Luke and his friends were ready to escape the Death Star. Smiling peacefully, he stopped fighting and closed his eyes.

With a swift motion, Vader swung his lightsaber, slicing through the spot where Obi-Wan stood! But the old Jedi vanished at that very instant, leaving nothing but his dusty cloak and weapon behind.

"No!" Luke shouted in horror.

The stormtroopers heard Luke shout and opened fire on the escaping rebels. Han and Chewie led Leia and the droids up the gangplank to the *Falcon* as more stormtroopers arrived. Luke stayed outside the ship, firing wildly. He no longer cared about his own safety. Suddenly, he heard Obi-Wan's voice in his head.

Run, Luke. Run!

Luke turned to board the *Falcon* just as Han and Chewie started the engines. With the tractor beam disabled, the ship raced away from the Death Star!

But the *Falcon* still had to get past the space station's sentry TIE fighters.

Leia and Chewbacca piloted the ship while Luke and Han handled the guns. The *Falcon* shook violently as blast after blast bounced off the ship.

As the *Falcon* got farther away from the Death Star, Luke and Han began to win the battle against the TIE fighters.

"Got him! I got him!" Luke yelled after blowing up another TIE. Soon Han and Luke had shot down all the remaining ships, and the *Falcon* entered hyperspace.

They were on their way to the rebel base at last. Truly, the Force was